NIKHIL AND JAY
THE STAR BIRTHDAY

To all the grandparents in our family
who love us unconditionally – CS

To Ibi, Yusuf, Mush and Maryam – S

Text copyright © Chitra Soundar 2021
Illustrations copyright © Soofiya 2021

First published in Great Britain in 2021 by
Otter-Barry Books, Little Orchard, Burley Gate,
Herefordshire, HR1 3QS
www.otterbarrybooks.com

A catalogue record for this book is available from the British Library.

ISBN 978-1-91307-461-6

Set in Sabon

Printed in Great Britain

9 8 7 6 5 4 3 2 1

NIKHIL AND JAY
THE STAR BIRTHDAY

Written by Chitra Soundar

Illustrated by Soofiya

Otter-Barry BOOKS

Grandad and Jay

Nikhil

Amma

Chennai Granny

Nana and Appa

Chennai Grandad

Max the Cat

CONTENTS

MANGO MADNESS

School was fun on Fridays. Nikhil had a whole period for drawing. It was Jay's turn to feed the school's pet hamster.

But this Friday morning was different. Nikhil and Jay wanted to stay at home. Grandad and Granny were coming from Chennai, in India.

"I can play and draw with Grandad," said Nikhil.

"I'll look after my toy hamster, Prince," said Jay. "My friends will feed the real one."

"No and no," said Amma. "You can see Grandad and Granny when you're back from school. They're going to be here all summer."

That was that.

All day at school, Nikhil and Jay couldn't wait to get home. At home-time, they had a surprise. Chennai Grandad came with Amma to collect them.

Grandad lifted Jay for a hug. "You're a big boy now!"

"Me too," said Nikhil.

"I'm so strong, I can lift both of you," said Grandad, lifting Nikhil up for a hug too.

On their way back, Nikhil told Grandad everything about school. Jay held up his rainbow-coloured toy hamster, Prince. "I have a real one in school too," he said.

Chennai Granny was waiting for them outside the house.

"This is the best Friday ever!" said Nikhil, running to her.

"Granny, this is Prince," shouted Jay, holding up his hamster.

After dinner with Chennai Granny and Grandad and a bedtime story from Granny, Nikhil and Jay couldn't wait for the weekend to begin.

When Jay woke on Saturday morning, he rushed down to see Granny and Grandad. "Shall we play Indian Ludo?" he asked.

"It's called dayam," said Granny, "but it's too early in the morning to be playing board-games."

After breakfast, Nikhil asked, "Will you teach us new Tamil songs?"

"Not early in the morning," said Grandad. "My throat needs to warm up."

"What are we going to do then?" asked Jay.

"We're going to the Indian market," said Amma.

The Indian market was not far from
their house. There were many shops with
vegetables, fruits and other food from India.
They bought paavai, a green vegetable that
was scaly like a crocodile.

"It tastes bitter too," said Amma.

"Like a crocodile?" asked Jay.

Then they bought a long green vegetable called the snake gourd.

"Is this bitter too?"

"No, this will be slimy," said Granny.

"Can we buy something that doesn't look like reptiles?" asked Nikhil.

"We're here to buy mangoes," said Grandad. "The fruit for gods."

"Are you a god?" asked Nikhil.

Granny laughed. "He wishes," she whispered as she looked for the perfect mangoes.

"I've chosen a dozen," said Granny, handing the mangoes to Appa.

"A dozen means 12," said Jay.

"I knew that already," said Nikhil. "Do you know how many is a baker's dozen?"

"I don't know," said Jay.

"13!" said Nikhil.

When they reached home, Appa said, "I'll chop up the mangoes for us."

"No! No!" cried Grandad. "No chopping up. Don't remove the skin either."

"How are we going to eat them, then?" asked Nikhil.

"Wait for it," said Granny. She broke off the stem on the top, washed the mangoes and handed out one each.

"Now watch," said Grandad.

He was just going to bite into it, but...

"No!" cried Amma. "Not on the carpet. You'll drip sticky juice all over it."

"Let's go to the dining room," said Jay.

Grandad and Nikhil followed Jay.

"No!" cried Appa. "I just mopped the floor this morning."

"Where are we going to eat, then?" asked Jay.

"Let's go into the garden," said Nikhil.

They all went to the garden. The smell of sweet mangoes invited bees and wasps towards them.

"No!" cried Grandad. "I don't want to be stung."

Max the Cat was sitting on the window-sill outside the bathroom. He mewed.

Nikhil looked up. "I've got an idea," he said. "Come with me."

They tiptoed through the dining room and the hallway, and climbed up the stairs.

Nikhil got into the bath-tub. Jay got in too.

"What a great idea," said Grandad.

Max the Cat watched them from the other side of the window.

Soon they finished eating their whole mangoes. They even scraped off the flesh from the pit.

"The mango peel has so many vitamins," said Grandad.

"What if it's bitter?" asked Jay.

"Granny picked out the sweetest ones for us," Grandad replied.

Amma and Appa brought their mangoes to the bath too. Then came Granny. Soon they had all finished eating.

"Wash your hands and face," said Amma.

"Now let's wash the bath," said Nikhil, spraying water everywhere.

"Hey, stop!" said Jay. "It's my turn."

Max the Cat jumped away. He definitely did not eat mangoes and he didn't need a bath.

STAR BIRTHDAY

It had been a week since Chennai Granny and Grandad had arrived. This Saturday morning, Nikhil was even more excited. His birthday was just a week away.

"Will you have a party?" asked Jay.

"Yes!" said Nikhil. "I've invited all my friends."

"What about my friends?" asked Jay.

"They'll come to YOUR birthday party," said Nikhil.

For breakfast, Granny placed plates full of idli before them.

"Ooh! I love idli," said Nikhil.

"Me too," said Jay. "Prince likes it too."

"Eat up, today is a special day," said Granny.

"Why?" asked Jay.

Max the Cat jumped on to a chair and waited. He wanted to know too.

"It's Nikhil's birthday today," she replied.

"No, it's not," said Nikhil.

"This is a special celebration," said Granny. "A Chennai birthday."

"Will Appa bake a cake?" asked Jay.

"No, Granny will make payasam," said Amma. "It's a milk pudding that you can drink."

Granny showed two packets to Nikhil. "This is vermicelli, straight and tall, and this is sago, white and round. What shall we add to your payasam?"

"Sago!" said Nikhil.

"That's my favourite too," said Amma.

Jay helped pick the best cashews for roasting. Then Granny poured milk into the pot for boiling.

Max the Cat came closer. *Anything that smells like milk is a good thing*, he thought.

"It's my birthday," said Nikhil. "What can I do?"

"Here! Crush the cardamom," said Granny.

"How?"

Granny handed Nikhil a mortar and pestle made of bronze. "Put the pod in here and press hard with the pestle," she said. "Don't ring  the mortar like a bell. Be quiet as a mouse."

Nikhil put the cardamom pod into the mortar and pressed it hard with the pestle.

When the green pod broke and the black cardamom seeds were crushed, Granny collected them in a little cup.

"Now I'll ring the bell," said Jay, hitting the mortar with the pestle.

Max the Cat scuttled out of the kitchen. He didn't like sudden noises.

Nikhil wondered if he would get presents in the Chennai celebration too?

Just as he was about to ask Granny about it, the payasam was ready.

Granny said a short prayer for Nikhil and all the elders blessed him.

"Can I bless him too?" asked Jay.

"You're not grown-up enough," said Nikhil.

"I'll bless Max the Cat and Prince the hamster," said Jay.

Max the Cat wasn't sure about that.

"One more thing," called Granny.

"Is it presents time?" asked Nikhil.

"Our blessings are our presents," said Grandad.

"But..."

"And this," said Granny, handing Nikhil a brown envelope.

Jay and Max the Cat came closer to look.

"Open it," she said.

Nikhil wasn't sure exciting things came in brown envelopes. "I'll open it," said Jay.

"It's my special birthday," said Nikhil. "I'll open it."

Inside was a five-pound note. "Whatever your heart wishes," said Granny.

Nikhil smiled. "I'll put it in my piggy bank," he said. "I'm saving up for an easel for art class."

"Wonderful idea," said Appa.

"Thank you, Granny and Grandad," said Nikhil, giving them a big hug.

"What about me?" asked Jay.

"You get our blessings too," said Grandad. "And a hug."

"What about money?" asked Jay.

"Oi!" said Amma.

"Look in your pocket," said Grandad, laughing.

A pound coin was there.

"Magic!" said Appa.

Granny clapped her hands. "Wash your hands and come to the table," she said. "Special treat coming up."

She placed a little steel tumbler filled with payasam in front of everyone.

"I need a spoon," said Nikhil. "The sago balls look like pearls floating in the sea."

"Drink the payasam and then dig for pearls," said Grandad. "That's what I always do."

"Why did we celebrate my birthday today?" asked Nikhil.

"Right!" said Granny, bringing a yellow book to the table. "This is the Tamil almanac. It tells us when the moon becomes full and when it disappears. We know which stars are travelling towards us and shine brightly."

"But..."

"Wait for it," said Amma.

"On the day Nikhil was born, a star called *Krithikai* sparkled bright in the sky. So every year, in the month Nikhil was born, we celebrate when the star returns to the sky."

"It's my star birthday," said Nikhil.

"Yes, it is," said Amma.

"Do I have a star too?" asked Jay.

"Of course," said Grandad. "But tonight, the brightest star in the sky will be Nikhil's."

That night, after Amma and Appa said good night, Nikhil whispered, "I'm going to stay awake and spot my star."

"Me too," said Jay.

But soon their eyes closed and they fell asleep. Only Max the Cat and Prince the hamster sat by the window, watched the sky, and saw the star.

A BANANA FEAST

The summer was hot. The house was full of grandparents – two sets of them.

Nikhil and Jay tried to play catch in the garden. But they kept getting caught in the washing.

"Let's play Cat on the Wall," said Jay.

"That's boring," said Nikhil. He didn't want to watch Max the Cat snoozing.

"Boring!" thought Max the Cat too. He wanted to play Chase the Bird.

"I wish we could go to the park," said Nikhil.

Jay ran inside to tell everyone.

"Let's go to the park," he shouted.

"Hey! That's my idea," said Nikhil.

"It's a great idea," said Amma. "Maybe we can have a picnic too."

Both the grandfathers went off to get blankets. Granny said she would cook all the Indian favourites. Nana said she would pack the fruit and sweets.

Appa filled all the steel water bottles with cold water from the tap.

Nikhil and Jay wanted to bring some things to the park too.

"What's all this?" asked Appa, when he saw a mountain of stuff stacked by the door.

"For the park," said Jay.

"Nope!" said Appa. "Just three things."

"Let's get the ball and the frisbee," said Nikhil.

"And our bikes," said Jay.

"That's four things," said Nikhil.

Nikhil and Jay were ready – but no one else was.

"Go help your grandmother!" said Appa.

"Which one?" asked Jay.

Appa laughed. "Whichever one needs help."

Chennai Granny was packing all the picnic food in plastic boxes.

"That's plastic," said Nikhil.

"Yeah, what to do?" said Granny. "In Chennai, we use steel tiffin boxes or banana leaves. I don't have those here."

"I can help," said Nikhil.

Nikhil dragged Jay to the garden and whispered, "We need to collect big leaves to pack food in. My teacher told us that plastic is peril."

"What is peril?"

"It means danger!"

"Like a crocodile?"

"Worse!" said Nikhil. "It's a monster that kills all the sea creatures."

So they looked at all the plants and trees in the garden. Some leaves were prickly and most were very small.

"Grandad!" shouted Jay. "Can you help us?"

Grandad came to find out what the problem was.

"Why can't we plant bananas in our garden?" asked Nikhil.

"Because they need a lot of sunshine," Grandad replied.

"But why do you need a banana plant?"

"To grow banana leaves," said Nikhil.

"So the plastic monster won't get us," said Jay.

"If only there was a shop for leaves," said Nikhil.

"Roar!" shouted Jay. "I'm a leaf monster. You can be the mango monster."

Mango! That reminded Nikhil of the Indian market.

"Grandad, will we find banana leaves in the Indian market?" he asked.

"Good thinking," said Grandad.

"I'll take you in my car, if you know the way," Grandpa said.

So two grandads and two grandsons went to the market to get banana leaves.

In the shop, Chennai Grandad showed them the banana stem. It was white and long.

"Your granny makes a great stir-fry with this," he said.

Then he picked up a purple banana flower.

"Can we eat this too?" asked Jay.

"Of course," said Grandad. "First you
have to pick each flower from the bunch.
Then Granny will chop it up and cook it with
lentils and chillies."

"What's this?" asked Nikhil.

"It's green banana," said Grandad. "We eat that too. Nothing is wasted from a banana plant. Look, this is a packet of banana chips, made from half-green, half-ripe bananas."

"Crisps?" asked
Grandpa.

"We call them chips
in Chennai," said
Grandad. "Banana
chips."

"I love chips," said
Jay.

They soon returned home with a banana
stem, a banana flower, two green bananas,
a bunch of yellow bananas, a packet of chips
and lots of banana leaves.

"What's all this?" asked Appa.

"A banana feast," said Nikhil.

Granny packed all the food she had made in banana leaves. Then she wrapped them in old newspapers and tied them with a cotton string. "See! No plastic," she said.

In the park, they had a wonderful morning – running, jumping, catching the frisbee and kicking the ball. Nikhil and Jay circled around the park on their bikes while Max the Cat snoozed on the warm grass.

Soon everyone was hungry.

Amma and Appa unpacked the food and handed everything out. Uh oh! How do you eat with forks and knives on banana leaves?

"My leaf will tear," said Nikhil.

"Eat with your fingers," said Amma. "Like Chennai folks do."

"It's hard," said Jay, trying to catch the rice between his fingers.

"It's easy," said Nikhil, picking up banana chips and putting them in his mouth.

Everybody laughed. Nikhil and Jay thought it was the best picnic ever.

SAYING GOODBYE

Summer was almost over. Granny helped Amma sew labels on to the boys' uniforms for the new school year. Grandad and Appa took Nikhil and Jay to get shoes.

"We'll be back in Chennai when school starts," said Grandad, as they tried on new shoes.

"You can stay here as long as you like," said Nikhil.

"Please don't go back," said Jay.

Grandad's eyes were full of tears as they got off the bus and walked home.

"What happened to all of you?" asked Granny. "You look like Max the Cat when the bird flew away."

"We don't want you and Grandad to go back to Chennai," said Nikhil.

"Not fair," said Jay.

Now Granny's eyes were full of tears too.

Nikhil and Jay went to their room and sat quietly.

"Hello," said Granny, peeping through the door. "Can we come in?"

Nikhil and Jay nodded.

"Are you going because I didn't share my cake with you?" asked Jay.

"Not at all," said Granny.

"Is it because I didn't listen to you yesterday?" asked Nikhil.

"Definitely not," said Grandad. "But it would be nice if you *did* listen to us."

"Then why?" wailed Nikhil.

Grandad sat on the bed next to Nikhil and put his arm around him. Granny sat on the floor and Jay cuddled up on her lap.

"We love you both very much," said
Grandad.

"Even more than we love your parents,"
said Granny, chuckling.

Jay giggled.

"But we have four coconut trees, two mango trees, a guava tree, a jasmine bush and many banana plants in our garden to look after," said Granny. "We miss our brothers and sisters and friends too."

Max the Cat purred.

"Do you have a cat?" asked Jay.

"No, but we have squirrels in the garden, a crow that comes to eat from our window, and sparrows that build nests in our trees."

"Maybe you can come and visit us in Chennai sometime," said Grandad.

"We'll come for Christmas," said Jay. "And I'll bring Prince too."

Nikhil counted on his fingers. "That's four months away," he said.

The post box rattled. Jay went to check.

"It's the postman," shouted Jay, "bringing letters for someone."

That gave Nikhil an idea. "Do you have a postman in Chennai?" he asked.

"Of course," said Granny. "He wears a khaki uniform and rides a bicycle."

"Will he bring a letter from us?"

"If you post them with stamps," said Grandad.

"Oh!" said Nikhil. "I don't know how to do that."

"I'll show you," said Grandad.

At the post-office, Grandad bought a pack of envelopes and a sheet of purple stamps.

"Who is this?" asked Jay, pointing at the stamps.

"That's the Queen," said Nikhil.

"I knew that," said Jay. "What's her name?"

"Queen Elizabeth the Second," said Nikhil.

When they came back home, Grandad wrote the Chennai address on four envelopes. "One for each month," he said.

Then Jay helped to peel off a stamp and stuck one on each of the four envelopes.

Nikhil wrote on the back of each envelope –
From Nikhil and Jay.

"Can I stick the envelope down now?" asked Jay.

"No, no," said Grandpa. "First you must write a letter and then put the paper inside the envelope before closing it."

Jay hugged Prince and turned away.

"What's wrong?" asked Granny.

"I'm not good at writing letters yet," said Jay.

"You're good at drawing," said Granny.

"Can I draw in the letter too?" asked Jay.

"Of course you can," she said. "And stick stickers too."

"Nik, Nik," shouted Jay. "I can draw and stick stickers too."

"I knew that," said Nikhil. "After we stick the envelope down, what do we do, Grandad?"

"Just drop it into any post box," said Grandad.

"There's one near our school," said Jay.

"I know that," said Nikhil. "But you can't reach it. So I'll post it."

"I can reach it when I'm older," said Jay.

"Then I'll reply to you," said Grandad, "and your postman will bring it and drop it through your letter box."

"Don't forget to write *From Grandad and Granny* on the back of the envelope," said Nikhil.

That night, when Grandad and Granny came to say good night, Nikhil said, "I'll write to you every month."

"Me too," said Jay. "We'll visit you."

"I'll miss you until then," said Nikhil.

"Me too," said Jay.

"We'll miss you too," said Grandad.

"And we love you loads," said Granny.

"Miaow!" said Max the Cat.

Nikhil and Jay's Guide to New Words

Chennai – a coastal city in India where our Amma's parents, Chennai Granny and Grandad, live.

Dayam – an ancient Indian board game played by kings and queens. Chennai Granny thinks Ludo was derived from this game.

Tamil – an ancient language spoken by people of Tamil Nadu, a state in India.

Paavai – a green and scaly vegetable grown in India. It's called bitter-gourd in English because it's very bitter.

Idli – steamed rice cake made with rice and lentil batter.

Vermicelli – a type of thin pasta, thinner than spaghetti. Chennai Granny calls it *semiya* in Tamil.

Sago – tiny pearls made of tapioca starch.
Chennai Granny calls it *Javvarisi* in Tamil.

Cardamom – a spice grown in India. It has a green shell and black seeds inside the shell.
Chennai Granny crushes the seeds and adds them in her tea and Indian puddings.

Payasam – an Indian milk pudding.
It's a bit runny, like milkshake.

Krithikai – one of the many stars in the sky, and each star has a story too.

Chennai Granny's Recipe for Sago Payasam

Try this recipe with the help of an adult!
Do not use the blender or the stove on your own.

Ingredients

- Cashew nuts – a few
- Raisins – golden or black – a few
- 100g sugar
- 100g sago
- 200ml milk
- 400ml water
- Cardamom – 2 cloves (or a pinch of cardamom powder)
- Ghee – 3 tablespoons

How to prepare the garnish

1. Heat two tablespoons of ghee in a wok.

2. Once the ghee is hot, add whole or broken cashews and sauté.

3. As they turn golden, add the raisins and sauté.

4. Turn off the heat when the raisins are plump. Remove from the ghee and keep aside.

5. Separately break the cardamom pods and crush them into a fine powder. You can also use cardamom powder.

How to Make the Payasam

1. In a pan, dry roast the sago pearls until they pop. Keep moving them around until they all pop.

2. Add the water and keep stirring until the sago pearls are cooked. When they are cooked, they turn translucent.

3. Pour the milk into it and stir well.

4. When it starts to thicken, reduce the heat.

5. Add the sugar and keep stirring on low heat until the sugar melts.

6. Now add the cardamom powder and stir well.

7. Add the remaining ghee and stir well.

8. Turn off the heat and add the cashew nuts and raisins. The sago payasam is ready!

Jay's tip: Add lots of crunchy cashews!

CHITRA SOUNDAR

Chitra Soundar is an author and storyteller, based in London, UK. She has been writing stories for a very long time. Although her family has appeared in many of her books (Shh! Don't tell them!), this is the first time she has written stories that are entirely inspired by her blended family, that follow the traditions of multiple heritages. Chitra is the author of many picture books, notably *Pattan's Pumpkin* (illustrated by Frané Lessac), also published by Otter-Barry Books. When not writing, Chitra enjoys walking, taking photos of flowers and spending time with her nephews. Find out more about her at www.chitrasoundar.com

SOOFIYA

Soofiya is a visual artist and illustrator.
Soofiya's work and writing explores ideas around
race, gender and bodies. Their illustrations and
design clients include Tate Britain, Mayor of London,
Hachette, BBC, Nike and many more. They currently
live close to the sea, and like to spend weekends
painting and taking care of their plants.
You can see more of their work here: soofiya.com

Read more about
NIKHIL AND JAY

ISBN 978-1-91307-462-3